The Case of the Disappearing Necklace

Sherlock Hound

Make friends with the most famous dog detective in town!

Be sure to read:

The Case of the Howling Armour

... and lots, lots more!

The Case of the Disappearing Necklace

Karen Wallace
illustrated by Emma Damon

SCHOLASTIC

To Jen, who follows things up – K.W.

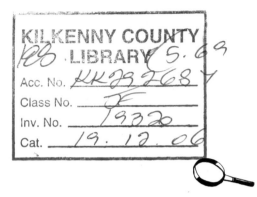

Scholastic Children's Books,
Commonwealth House, 1-19 New Oxford Street,
London, WC1A 1NU, UK
a division of Scholastic Ltd
London ~ New York ~ Toronto ~ Sydney ~ Auckland
Mexico City ~ New Delhi ~ Hong Kong

First published by Scholastic Ltd, 2002

ISBN 0 439 99447 0

Printed and bound by Oriental Press, Dubai, UAE

10 9 8 7 6 5 4 3 2

Chapter One

Sherlock Hound, famous dog detective, was eating his breakfast bone and reading his newspaper when there was a *rat-ta-ta-tat* on the door.

A minute later, his loyal friend,
Dr WhatsUp Wombat, ran into the room.
"What's up, Dr Wombat?" growled the
famous dog detective.

If there was one thing Sherlock Hound
hated, it was being disturbed at breakfast.

"Someone has broken into the Egyptian Museum!" cried Dr WhatsUp Wombat. "They've robbed the tomb of Queen Dirtifeeti!"

Sherlock Hound put down his paper and looked thoughtful. "And the only things missing are her emerald earrings," he said slowly.

"How did you know?" gasped Dr WhatsUp Wombat.

"Queen Dirtifeeti is famous for two

things," replied Sherlock Hound, "her smelly feet and her magic emerald jewellery."

He went over to the bookcase and pulled out a very old book. It was called:

Stinky Queens of Egypt

In the middle were two pictures. In one, Queen Dirtifeeti wore an emerald necklace and thick bandages on her feet. She was holding a pair of emerald earrings.

In the other, there was nothing.

Queen Dirtifeeti had disappeared!

"Whoever wears the emerald earrings and the emerald necklace at the same time can make themselves disappear," explained Sherlock Hound.

He looked serious. "Did you find any clues at the museum?"

"Only this."

Dr WhatsUp Wombat opened his battered briefcase and held out a long grey bandage.

Sherlock Hound wrinkled his nose.

The bandage smelled of very old feet.
He picked up his magnifying glass and
peered through it.

"This bandage has been chewed," said
Sherlock Hound. "And there's only one
person who could do such a disgusting
thing."

Dr WhatsUp Wombat looked pale.
"Professor Ha-ha Hyena," he whispered.

"Exactly, my dear Doctor," said Sherlock
Hound. "Professor Ha-ha Hyena, master of
disguise and the most evil
criminal in the world!"

Dr WhatsUp Wombat stared at Sherlock Hound. "Do you think Professor Ha-ha Hyena has stolen the emerald earrings to make himself disappear?"

"Most certainly," replied Sherlock Hound. "At tea-time today, the Bank of England moves all its gold to a top-secret hiding place. Now, if that evil hyena was invisible, he could find out the hiding place and no one would know!"

Dr WhatsUp Wombat gulped. "And where is the necklace?"

"It belongs to a wannabe movie star called Delicious Dolores Douglas," replied Sherlock Hound. "Her daddy, Lotsa Dough Douglas, gave it to her for her birthday."

"Then we must find the necklace before Professor Ha-ha Hyena," cried Dr WhatsUp Wombat. "But where shall we look?"

Sherlock Hound picked up his newspaper and pointed to a picture of a tubby blonde woman on the front page. She was standing on the steps of the Glitz Hotel.

THE DAILY NEWS

DELICIOUS DOLORES COMES TO TOWN

Sherlock Hound grabbed his special travelling cloak and hurried to the door. "I think we should pay Delicious Dolores a visit!"

In her enormous room in the Glitz Hotel,
Delicious Dolores hummed a happy tune as
she squeezed into a short, shiny green dress.

She clipped on the funny-looking green necklace her daddy had given her.

Then she gave herself a big kiss in the mirror. "You're going to be a movie star!" she squealed.

She wiggled out of the door and took the VIP see-through lift to the ground floor.

Sherlock Hound squeezed his eyes shut. He hated heights, so going up in the VIP see-through lift at the Glitz Hotel was not his favourite thing.

Suddenly Dr WhatsUp Wombat gasped.

A tubby blonde woman in a tight green dress was passing them on the way down! It was Delicious Dolores and she was wearing the emerald necklace!

"She's going out," cried Dr WhatsUp Wombat. "What are we going to do?"

"Search her room for clues," replied Sherlock Hound.

Chapter Three

Sherlock Hound stood in Delicious Dolores's room and stared at a strange piece of paper. It had a furry black and yellow stripe around the edge.

He read out the message.

Dear Miss Dolores,
You are going to be a
Movie star!
I want you to have the
biggest part in my next movie.
Meet me for lunch at the
Fanciest Restaurant in Town.
Your biggest fan,
xx Garry Grabbit III
(Famous Movie Director)
P.S Wear green.
It's my favourite colour.

"There's only one person who would have a furry black and yellow stripe around their notepaper," muttered Sherlock Hound. "And his name isn't Garry Grabbit III."

Sherlock Hound gritted
his teeth. If there was
one thing he hated, it
was fancy restaurants.

They were a waste of
time and a waste of money.
And they never served spaghetti hoops.
But a dog's gotta do what a dog's gotta do!

Two minutes later, he climbed into a taxi
beside Dr WhatsUp. "Take us to the
Fanciest Restaurant
in Town," he
growled.

Professor Ha-ha Hyena leaned back in his chair. There was nothing he liked better than fancy restaurants.

They were a waste of time and a waste of money. And they never served spaghetti hoops.

Professor Ha-ha Hyena felt in his pocket for Queen Dirtifeeti's magic emerald earrings. Everything was going according to plan!

All he needed was the
necklace and by tea-time
all the Bank of England's
gold would be his!

"Cooee! Garry Grabbit!" Delicious
Dolores wiggled across
the floor and held out
her hand. She looked
like a pink and
green wedding
cake on stilts.

"Darling! Darling!" cried Professor Ha-ha
Hyena. He took Delicious Dolores's pudgy
pink hand and gave her a kiss.

"You look WONDERFUL!" he purred.
"And what a beautiful green necklace!"
"I wore it specially for you!" squealed

Delicious Dolores.

She threw herself down on a thin gold chair. "Now, what's for lunch?"

"Anything your pretty heart desires," murmured Professor Ha-ha Hyena.

"Yummy!" cried Delicious Dolores. "I'm starving!"

As Professor Ha-ha Hyena peered at the enormous menu, Sherlock Hound and Dr WhatsUp Wombat sneaked past to a nearby table.

The evil professor never knew they were there!

Chapter Four

Two hours later, Delicious Dolores was still eating!

"What can we do?"
whispered Dr
WhatsUp
Wombat.

"Wait,"
murmured
Sherlock Hound.
He looked at his watch. "Don't forget, the
professor needs the necklace by tea-time."

"More caviar, madam?" murmured a
waiter, holding out a ladle full of tiny black
wobbly things.

Delicious Dolores's eyes lit up. "Yethe pleathe," she said, with her mouth full. "Then I'll have roathe beef."

Across the table, Professor Ha-ha Hyena was getting worried.

Caviar was only the first course! And it was almost tea-time!

He had to steal the necklace before the Bank of England moved the gold!

There was only
one thing to do.
Very slowly and very
gently, the professor
pulled out his watch
and chain. His eyes
glittered as the watch
swung back and forth,
back and forth over the white tablecloth.

Delicious Dolores
looked up from
her bowl.

"You're getting sleepy," murmured
Professor Ha-ha Hyena.

Delicious Dolores stared and said nothing.

"Very sleepy," murmured the professor.

A blob of caviar
dribbled down
Delicious
Dolores's chin.
And her eyes rolled
back in her head.

"Give me the necklace," murmured Professor Ha-ha Hyena.

Delicious Dolores nodded and began to hand over the necklace.

Chapter Five

Across the room, Sherlock Hound and
Dr WhatsUp Wombat put down their
silly little ice-cream spoons.

They watched as Professor Ha-ha Hyena
fastened the emerald necklace around his
own neck.

"Wait until he gets out the earrings," growled the famous dog detective.

Seconds later, a nasty smirk spread across Professor Ha-ha Hyena's spotty furry face. Then he reached into his pocket and pulled out the earrings.

"Now!" cried Sherlock Hound.

He raced towards his enemy.

At the same moment, a waiter carrying
a huge silver dome glided across the
restaurant towards Professor Ha-ha Hyena
and Delicious Dolores.

Dr WhatsUp Wombat gasped.

The waiter was going to bump right into Sherlock Hound!

Dr WhatsUp Wombat did the first thing he could think of.

He picked up a scoop of strawberry ice cream and threw it at the waiter.

SPLAT! The gooey pink ball hit the waiter right in the face.

BONG! The huge silver dome crashed to the floor! A lump of roast beef, dozens of potatoes and hundreds of peas rolled all over the place!

Professor Ha-ha Hyena jumped up in surprise. Sherlock Hound was standing right in front of him!

"You'll never escape!" growled Sherlock Hound.

Professor Ha-ha Hyena hooted with laughter. "Watch me, you flea-ridden mongrel!" he cried.

Then quick as a flash, he clipped on an earring.

Chapter Six

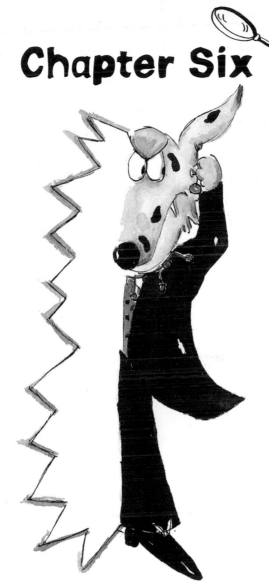

Sherlock Hound's heart went BANG in his chest! Half of Professor Ha-ha Hyena had disappeared! Any second now he would become completely invisible!

There was a glint of green as the evil
hyena held up the other earring.

"Not so fast!" shouted Sherlock Hound.

THUMP! SPLAT! The famous dog
detective leaped at Professor Ha-ha Hyena
and they fell back into a pool of black
wobbly caviar!

"Give me that earring!" cried Sherlock
Hound.

"Never," snarled Professor Ha-ha Hyena. He snapped the other earring to his ear just as Sherlock Hound pulled the emerald necklace from his neck!

As Professor Ha-ha Hyena felt himself reappear, he let out a howl of fury.

At the sound of the howl, Delicious Dolores woke up! "Give me back my necklace!" she shouted. She grabbed the necklace from Sherlock Hound.

"And I'll have those earrings, too!" She snatched the earrings from the evil professor.

"Madam! Wait!" cried Dr WhatsUp Wombat.

"Why should I?" yelled Delicious Dolores. "You're a bunch of crooks and you want to stop me being a movie star!"

With that, she snapped on Queen
Dirtifeeti's emerald
jewellery and
disappeared.

There was only one thing to do!
Sherlock Hound grabbed
the huge silver dome and
banged it down on
top of the invisible
Delicious Dolores.
It was the only
way to stop
her escaping!

Ouch!

In that second, Professor Ha-ha Hyena saw his chance.

"You'll never catch me now," he howled. And he shot through the revolving doors in a whirl of fur.

Back at 221b Barker Street, Sherlock
Hound poured out two mugs of cocoa.

"How did you get the emeralds back?"
asked Dr WhatsUp Wombat.

"Easy peasy," replied Sherlock Hound.
"I let Delicious Dolores eat everything on
the menu, then I told her there were no jobs
for fat, invisible movie stars."

Dr WhatsUp Wombat stirred his cocoa. "And Professor Ha-ha Hyena?"

Sherlock Hound, famous dog detective, sat down in his favourite chair. "We'll get him next time," he said with a smile.